You are in a country that has many strange animals.
You have just seen the strangest of all.
It has a bill like a duck and webbed feet, but is covered with fur.
What is it ? No!—It is not a duck with a fur coat!
(See page 33.)

You are watching a race between an ostrich,
a horse, a gazelle, and a cheetah.
Who will win? Who'll be second? Third? Last?
(See page 12.)

You are up in the Arctic and a
one-ton, two-tusked walrus goes floating by.
What are those long tusks for?
(See page 19.)

to Holly and Will

Joe Kaufman's

WINGS
PAWS
HOOFS
AND
FLIPPERS

A BOOK ABOUT ANIMALS

Written and Illustrated by JOE KAUFMAN

EDWARD R. RICCIUTI, *Consultant*
Formerly of the New York Zoological Society

Golden Press • New York
Western Publishing Company, Inc. Racine, Wisconsin

Long ago, people thought
that dragons and many
other fantastic beasts
really existed.

CONTENTS

*A NOTE TO PARENTS: This book has been designed to show children the amazing variety of mammal and bird life.
Through his accurate and fun illustrations and thoroughly readable text, the author conveys much information and answers
many of the questions that children have a way of asking: which camels have two humps and which have one? How can you tell
the difference between African and Asian elephants? Which animal can run the fastest? The book is intended for children
from 6 to 12 years old, but will appeal to anyone who is interested in animals.*

And people believed that the oceans
were filled with frightening sea monsters.

EARLY IDEAS

EARLY IDEAS cave people had about animals were quite correct, because cave people hunted animals for food and learned much about the way wild creatures lived. Early people painted accurate pictures of animals on the walls of their caves. Later, when horses had been taught to carry a rider or pull a wagon, and sea-going ships had been developed, people began to travel far from home. They began to be afraid of meeting unknown and dangerous animals and then came to believe that such animals really existed.

The scary beasts people thought up were often combinations of parts of real animals. One such animal was the dragon, which had scales, a forked tongue like a snake, and claws like an eagle. The dragon was said to breathe fire.

Another legendary beast was the hydra, a snake with seven heads. If a head was cut off, according to the story, it grew back. Just as strange was the basilisk, an animal with the body of a reptile and a rooster's head. Its glance and breath were said to be fatal. The centaur was half horse and half man.

The great sea serpent, the half-fish merman, the unicorn sea monster, and the orc, with a fish's body and boar's head, were some of the strange beasts that people imagined living in the ocean.

Today, people have explored most of the earth's lands and some of its oceans. Scientists called zoologists, biologists, and ornithologists have learned many things about animals and the way they live all over the world. Some of what they have learned is in this book.

3¼ billion years ago one-celled life appeared in the sea. Jellyfish came later.

By 300 million years ago, there were starfish, lungfish, and amphibians.

150 million years ago dinosaurs and other reptiles roamed the land. Winged reptiles flew above.

The TYRANNOSAURUS, 50 feet long, weight 8 tons, was the giant of the meat-eaters.

crest

the PARASAUROLOPHUS, one of the duck-billed, crested dinosaurs

The DIPLODOCUS was the longest dinosaur— about 90 feet long.

The STEGOSAURUS, a vegetarian, had plates on its back for protection.

Not all dinosaurs were huge. The COMPSOGNATHUS was only as big as a chicken.

DINOSAURS and other reptiles dominated the earth for more than 200 million years. There were many kinds of these reptiles, different in appearance and habits.

The fiercest dinosaur was *Tyrannosaurus*. It had powerful hind legs for running and leaping, but small forelegs. Its head was huge. *Tyrannosaurus* killed and ate other reptiles with its mighty jaws and long, sharp teeth.

Parasaurolophus ate plants. Its crest probably had long nasal passages which increased its sense of smell. *Diplodocus* also fed on plants. It needed lots of them—its body weighed 15 tons—so it probably spent much of the day eating. *Compsognathus* ate insects and smaller reptiles. *Stegosaurus* had sharp spikes on its tail.

About 70 million years ago, dinosaurs and many other reptiles died out.

8

million years ago
[dino]saurs were gone and
[ma]mmals and birds had
[sp]read everywhere.

By 10 million years
ago, mammals and birds
were beginning to look
like those living today.

And finally...at long
last...a mere 100,000
or so years ago...
came Homo
sapiens...folks
much like
us...modern
PEOPLE!!!

The BALUCHITHERIUM, a giant plant-eater,
was the biggest land mammal
that ever existed.

The ARSINOITHERIUM
was probably
a plant-eater.

The HOPLOPHONEUS
was a saber-tooth cat
the size of a tiger.

EOHIPPUS had
spread-out toes to help
it walk on the ground.

The woolly MAMMOTH
had very long tusks
and a thick, hairy coat.

MAMMALS evolved from certain reptiles other than dinosaurs at least 180 million years ago.

Mammals are different from reptiles in many ways. One is that mammals feed their young on milk. Another is that mammals have hair.

Early mammals were smaller than a house cat; only after dinosaurs were gone did mammals become bigger. When there were no large reptiles to eat them, many kinds of mammals developed.

The *Baluchitherium* was a giant prehistoric rhinoceros. Its head was 4½ feet long. The woolly mammoth was a prehistoric relative of the elephant. It lived in cold climates, where its long, hairy coat kept it warm. The earliest horse, *Eohippus*, was not much bigger than a cat. *Arsinotherium* had four horns and was very large. Scientists do not know if it is related to any modern animals. The *Hoplophoneus* was a huge cat.

9

The house cat is part of the cat family. It is the only domesticated one of the family. The rest of its relatives are wild.

DOMESTIC CATS, or house cats, look and act very much like their wild relatives.

All cats have characteristics that make them good hunters. For instance, the ability of a cat's eye to reflect whatever light is available helps the cat see at night. Its whiskers serve as feelers, helping it get around in the dark and in narrow places. A cat can hear very high-pitched sounds such as the squeaks of its prey. The cat can extend its claws to climb, and pull them in to creep along silently on its padded feet. A cat has good balance, which helps it get around in trees and on roofs or fences. If a cat falls, it is likely to land on its feet. People say that cats have "nine lives," but this isn't really true; cats are just very good at getting out of trouble.

After a meal, a house cat cleans itself carefully and purrs like small wild cats.

House cats were developed from small tamed wild cats. The first house cats probably were bred in China, Egypt, and India and then brought to other countries by traders and sailors.

There are dozens of breeds of domestic cats, differing from each other in size, weight, and color. Persian and Himalayan cats have long, fluffy hair. Abyssinian, Manx, Russian Blue, Rex, and Siamese cats have short hair. The Siamese has beautiful blue eyes and also is known for its loud yowls.

Although there are many variations in the breeds of cats, these differences are slight compared to those that exist between breeds of dogs. Think of what a Saint Bernard looks like standing next to a tiny chihuahua! Most cats you are likely to see do not belong to fancy breeds but are mixes of different breeds. They still make wonderful pets.

Cats have been bred in most parts of the world, so that now, when cats are such popular pets, there is a great variety to choose from.

TURKISH cats were the first long-haired cats in Europe and America.

SIAMESE cats were developed by the family of the King of Siam.

PERSIAN cats come in many colors, including white, black, blue, brown, red, and gray.

ABYSSINIAN cats are thought to be the descendants of ancient Egyptian cats.

RUSSIAN Blue cats were brought by sailors from Russia to Britain.

BURMESE cats, raised in the temples of Burma, were believed to be sacred.

And here come some kittens:

calico   black short-hair   tabby   Manx   tortoise-shell

11

The PUMA is a good climber.

The LYNX lives where there are snowy winters.

NORTH AMERICA

The BOBCAT yowls loudly at night.

The JAGUAR is the third largest cat.

SOUTH AMERICA

The OCELOT hunts in trees and on the ground.

WILD CATS, big and small, live on every continent but Australia and Antarctica. All, whatever their size, are excellent hunters. They see very well, even in dim light, and have well-developed senses of smell and hearing. They are quick and agile.

The fastest cat is the cheetah. For a short distance it can run up to 70 miles an hour—it is faster than any other land animal. *

Lions live in open country. They travel around in groups called prides. Females care for the young and do most of the hunting. The males, some weighing more than 400 pounds, defend them from other prides. Each pride has its own home territory.

Tigers are big, too. Some are even larger than lions. Tigers live in forests in countries as hot as India and as cold as snowy Siberia. They are fine swimmers.

Leopards, smaller than lions and tigers, are nevertheless very strong. They climb well and often take the animals they kill into trees to eat them.

Jaguars live in Central and South America. Like leopards, they have spots. They are strong enough to kill caymans, cousins of alligators.

Pumas, also called mountain lions or cougars, live from Canada to the tip of South America. They keep away from people, so are hardly ever seen.

Lynxes have large tufts of fur on their ears. One type lives in northern Europe and North America. It has broad paws that help keep it from sinking into the snow. The caracal is a relative of the lynx. It roams the hot deserts and plains of Africa and Asia.

Ocelots are spotted cats of medium size which look like small jaguars. They live from the southwestern border of the United States to South America.

* *A gazelle runs 50 miles an hour.*
A racehorse runs 45 miles an hour.
An ostrich runs 35 miles an hour.

The LYNX lives in forests.

The EUROPEAN WILDCAT looks like a domestic cat.

The LYNX has thick fur for warmth.

The SIBERIAN TIGER has longer, paler fur than tigers in southern Asia.

The SPANISH LYNX has dark spots.

EUROPE

ASIA

The BLACK PANTHER— a spotted leopard born black.

The CARACAL is long-legged and speedy.

The LEOPARD lives in Asia and Africa.

The BENGAL TIGER is smaller than the Siberian.

The CHEETAH hunts gazelles.

AFRICA

Only the lion, the tiger, the jaguar, and the leopard can roar, but they can't purr very well.

The male LION is the only cat that has a mane, but not all male lions have one.

13

Long ago, before people developed different breeds of dogs, all dogs looked pretty much like this one.

The COLLIE originally was bred to care for sheep.

The BULLDOG, in spite of its huge jaw and fierce expression, is a gentle dog. Yet it was originally bred to fight bulls.

The DACHSHUND was developed to hunt badgers. With its long body and short legs, it can follow a badger into its hole.

POODLES are smart enough to do circus tricks.

DOMESTIC DOGS were first developed as working animals, not as pets. Breeds such as bloodhounds and beagles with a keen sense of smell were produced to hunt animals by following their trails. Other breeds such as greyhounds and whippets are used to track animals by sight. Some breeds such as pointers and setters combine both these qualities.

Dogs such as the sheltie, the collie, and the sheep dog herd cattle and sheep. Others, such as the husky, pull sleds.

Only pure breeds are shown in dog shows. Then there are mixed breeds, or "mutts," which, along with purebred dogs, live with humans as pets.

How is a new breed produced? Here is an example. Long ago, people needed a dog to hunt badgers and weasels, which live in holes. Big hunting dogs could not squeeze into the holes after the animals.

Could elephants also be bred for special purposes?

Could a very long elephant be developed for carrying many people?

long trunk for carrying luggage

Could elephants with tusks like spears have been bred to help knights in battle?

14

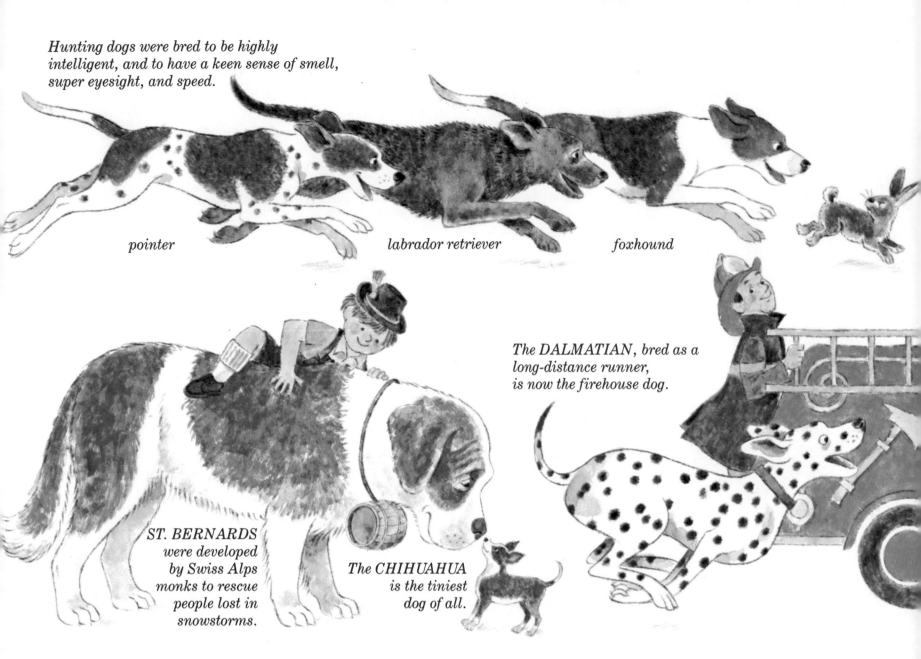

Hunting dogs were bred to be highly intelligent, and to have a keen sense of smell, super eyesight, and speed.

pointer   *labrador retriever*   *foxhound*

ST. BERNARDS were developed by Swiss Alps monks to rescue people lost in snowstorms.

The CHIHUAHUA is the tiniest dog of all.

The DALMATIAN, bred as a long-distance runner, is now the firehouse dog.

Breeders wanted a dog with a long, narrow body and short, strong legs for digging. So breeders looked for puppies with short legs, long bodies, or better yet, both. When the puppies grew up, they were mated with one another. Each time new puppies were born, breeders picked out those with the right kind of legs and body and kept them for mating. Years passed. The puppies that were born be-

came more and more like the dog the breeders wanted. Finally, all the puppies had the same kind of long, short-legged bodies. A new type of dog had been created—that sausage-shaped, short-legged wonder—the dachshund.

Best of all, most dogs make wonderful pets. They quickly learn their names, are friendly, and greet you by wagging their tails.

If there were breeders of elephants, could they develop elephants with short trunks? long hair? with spots?

And could these breeders produce a breed of darling little pet elephants?

15

WOLVES AND FOXES are part of a family of animals that also includes coyotes, jackals, and several other dog-like animals sometimes called "wild dogs." They are all wild relatives of domestic dogs. One or another of this family lives on every continent but Antarctica.

Wolves are the biggest animals of this group. They sometimes weigh more than 150 pounds and stand more than 3 feet high at the shoulder. Only a few domestic dogs—the Great Dane, for instance—reach this size.

Wolves stay with the same mate for life, and the father and mother take care of their cubs together. Wolves live in groups called packs. When the pack hunts, the members take turns chasing their prey until it tires.

Some foxes are as large as middle-sized dogs. Foxes are known as clever animals because they are

FOXES are mainly night hunters. They hunt alone, not in packs.

WOLVES, big and strong enough to hunt the largest of the deer family, will rarely attack people.

HYENAS look like dogs, but really are a family of their own. They live in Africa and Asia. They hunt for food and also eat the remains of animals other animals have killed.

spotted hyena

JACKALS hunt for small animals, but mostly eat the remains of dead ones.

excellent hunters and also are good at escaping from larger animals.

Coyotes look like small wolves. They live throughout much of North America. Coyotes howl at night in an eerie way.

Jackals live in Asia and Africa. They often eat the leftovers of a lion's meal.

Africa's Cape hunting dogs hunt like wolves. They eat animals such as zebras and antelopes.

COYOTES usually weigh about half as much as wolves. They eat dead animals they find, but usually kill their own prey.

CAPE HUNTING DOGS hunt in packs of as many as several dozen dogs.

GIANT PANDAS, about 5 feet tall and weighing up to 400 pounds, look like bears but are probably related to raccoons.

LESSER PANDAS look much like raccoons but have reddish fur.

RACCOONS eat plants, meat, and fish. They look for food at night.

RACCOONS and their cousins, such as coatis and kinkajous, live in the Americas. They have very sharp teeth. They use their forepaws much like hands—sometimes they dunk their food in water and seem to be washing it. These animals are at home both on the ground and in trees. In Asia there are two animals probably related to raccoons—the giant and lesser pandas. The giant panda is as big as a bear.

17

Most animals walk and stand on their toes, but bears walk with the sole and heel of the foot touching the ground. So do you.

bear's heel

dog's heel

The SLOTH BEAR eats mostly termites. Its claws are long, the better to tear open termite nests.

The Malayan SUN BEAR is the smallest of the bear family. It usually weighs under 100 pounds.

The SPECTACLED BEAR is the only bear living in South America.

The North American BLACK BEAR lives from Mexico to northern Canada. It is about as big as a large man.

The POLAR BEAR has thick fur to protect it from Arctic cold. Even the soles of its feet are furry.

This BROWN BEAR is in its winter sleep, but it is not hibernating.

BEARS have powerful legs, thick fur, a large head, and small eyes and ears. They usually walk on all fours, but can also walk on their hind legs. Bears look clumsy and slow, but they can run fast. All bears swim well, especially the polar bear, which sometimes paddles many miles out to sea. Bears also hear well and have an excellent sense of smell. Their eyesight is not very sharp.

Bears eat berries, grubs, fish, mice, and sometimes bigger animals such as deer. Some bears, such as the grizzly, are very fierce and will attack people.

Bears sleep deeply during much of the winter, but they do not really hibernate. When an animal hibernates, its breathing, digestion, and heartbeat almost stop. Bears may wake up, move around, and eat during the winter.

Adult HARP SEALS have harp-like markings. Pups are pure white.

ELEPHANT SEALS weigh up to 4 tons. They get their name because of their trunk-like snouts.

The Northern FUR SEAL breeds near Alaska.

The WALRUS digs its long tusks into the ice to help pull its heavy body out of the water.

SEALS AND WALRUSES live mostly in the water. They are mammals and need to breathe air, so they have to come up to the surface every so often. Their young are born out of water on ice floes or rocks. Seals and walruses usually live in big groups. Some seals are called "earless" because the outer part of their ears is not visible.

Seals are clumsy on land. They can't really walk, but push themselves along with their flippers. The rear flippers of the earless seals trail behind them and are of little use on shore. Fur seals, sea lions, and walruses have rear flippers that face forward, so they can get around more easily.

Walruses sometimes weigh more than a ton. Most spend their lives in icy Arctic waters. Their blubber keeps them warm.

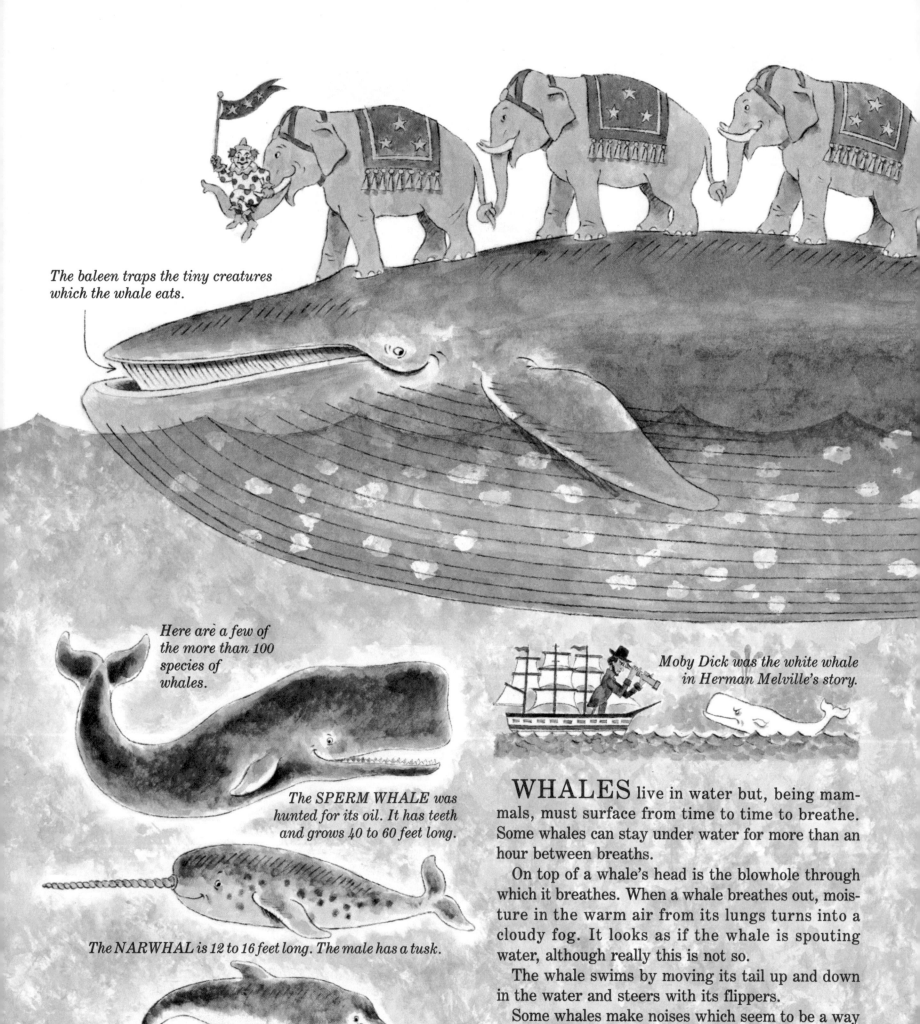

The baleen traps the tiny creatures which the whale eats.

Here are a few of the more than 100 species of whales.

Moby Dick was the white whale in Herman Melville's story.

The SPERM WHALE was hunted for its oil. It has teeth and grows 40 to 60 feet long.

The NARWHAL is 12 to 16 feet long. The male has a tusk.

The playful DOLPHIN is 6 to 12 feet long.

WHALES live in water but, being mammals, must surface from time to time to breathe. Some whales can stay under water for more than an hour between breaths.

On top of a whale's head is the blowhole through which it breathes. When a whale breathes out, moisture in the warm air from its lungs turns into a cloudy fog. It looks as if the whale is spouting water, although really this is not so.

The whale swims by moving its tail up and down in the water and steers with its flippers.

Some whales make noises which seem to be a way

20

The BLUE WHALE is the biggest animal of all.
It is bigger than any other animal that ever lived.
It can grow to be almost 100 feet long and weigh 130 tons.
A 6-ton elephant is tiny by comparison.

A whale mother gives birth to one baby at a time. Twins are very rare. The mother nurses the baby. The baby doesn't have to suck; the milk squirts into its mouth.

of "talking" to one another. Whales can hear sounds made by other whales miles away.

The skeleton of the whale shows that its ancestors were land animals. Whales don't have hind legs, but bones that supported their land ancestors' hind legs remain. The flippers contain bones from the fore-limb that look like those of an arm and hand.

There are two groups of whales—baleen whales and toothed whales. Baleen whales get their name from the long, flat strips (called baleen) which they have instead of teeth. The baleen acts as a strainer, filtering swarms of tiny sea creatures out of the water which the whale takes into its mouth. Baleen whales include the blue whale, the humpback whale, the right whale, and the finback whale. Baleen whales have two blowholes.

Toothed whales include the sperm whale, the beluga, the narwhal, and dolphins and porpoises. Toothed whales eat fish and squid. Some also feed on seals, sea birds such as penguins, and even other whales. The killer whale, really a giant dolphin, is the most fearsome of such hunters, and has been known to kill and eat large sea lions. Toothed whales have one blowhole.

The PROBOSCIS has a very long, fleshy nose and is expert at leaping from higher branches to lower ones. It often drops into a stream for a swim.

Sam, a RHESUS monkey "astronaut," rode in space before any human did.

The LANGUR monkey is a leaf-eater. Leaves aren't too nourishing so the langur eats huge quantities.

The MANGABEY is a thin, fruit-eating monkey that hides shyly up in the trees.

The RHESUS monkey is believed to be sacred by some people in India, so it is protected there.

BABOON females are much smaller than males. Babies ride on the mother's back.

The MANDRILL has a brightly colored face and is very strong and fierce.

OLD WORLD MONKEYS live in Africa and Asia. Separated for millions of years, the monkeys of Africa and Asia and those of the Americas became different from one another. The Old World monkeys have narrow, close-together nostrils. Some have cheek pouches for holding fruit, nuts, or other food until eaten. Most Old World monkeys have thick pads of skin on their rumps which often are brightly colored. Their hands resemble those of a human's—the thumb and fingers can be held opposite one another and so can grasp things tightly between them. Some Old World monkeys live in trees, others on the ground.

Like all monkeys, Old World monkeys live in groups of a few to many hundred. The smaller groups are families, the larger ones are gatherings of families. Monkeys like to clean or groom one another's fur. A monkey sits quietly while another monkey searches and picks through its hair, cleaning out dirt and bits of dead skin.

The PIGMY MARMOSET is the tiniest monkey and can fit in a man's cupped hand.

The SQUIRREL monkey cannot hang by its tail.

a Capuchin in costume

The UAKARI has a hairless face and a short tail, unusual for a New World monkey.

The CAPUCHIN monkey is very intelligent and was used by organ-grinders to collect money.

The HOWLER monkey's call can be heard for miles and probably warns other howler groups away from its territory.

The SPIDER monkey has long, skinny arms and legs that give it a spidery look when it hangs by its tail. It has little or no thumbs.

The WOOLLY monkey lives high in jungle trees and likes to eat fruit and leaves.

NEW WORLD MONKEYS live

in Central and South America. Their nostrils are round and well separated. They don't have cheek pouches for storing food, or pads on their rumps. They can't use their thumbs for grasping and can't hold things very well. Many, however, have a tail that grasps, known as a "prehensile" tail. It is used like an extra hand for grasping objects that are hard to reach, and also for holding on to branches or swinging from them. New World monkeys live in trees. Some never come down to the ground.

Like all monkeys, New World monkeys usually have one baby at a time. The newborn monkey clings to its mother with its hands and feet. She hugs it tightly to keep it safe until she feels it is strong enough to try things on its own. The mother nurses the baby for many months.

Monkeys make lots of noise "talking" to one another as they sit or feed in the trees. Some have loud voices that can be heard far away.

GIBBONS are the smallest apes. They are about 3 feet tall and weigh about 20 pounds.

Long-armed GIBBONS can balance upright and race along narrow branches and vines.

Hooking their fingers over branches, GIBBONS swing with ease.

GORILLAS are bigger than any other ape or monkey. They usually stay on the ground, but at times build nests in trees for sleeping.

APES look somewhat like monkeys but really are quite different. Most apes are bigger than any monkey. While monkeys are smart, apes are much smarter. Monkeys scamper through trees on all fours, while apes use their long, strong arms to swing and pull themselves through the branches. No ape has a tail.

Of all animals, apes are most like people, with similar muscles, bones, hands, and feet—even the same number of teeth, 32. But people have a bigger and better-developed brain than apes do. People

At birth a GORILLA weighs between 4 and 5 pounds, less than most newborn people.

GORILLAS walk or run on all fours, using their feet and the knuckles of their bent hands.

The mother ORANG-UTAN nurses her baby for several years.

Male ORANG-UTANS develop cheek flaps and a throat pouch.

Young ORANG-UTANS swing, climb, and play in the trees.

also stand straighter than apes and have longer legs than arms. Apes have longer arms than legs.

There are four main kinds of apes. One is the gibbon of southern Asia. Gibbons are even more at home in trees than monkeys are. They like the highest crowns of the tallest trees in the jungle. Gibbons weigh about 25 pounds.

Orang-utans also live in southern Asia. They weigh more than 200 pounds and they also live in trees. Gibbons and orang-utans eat many different things, including fruit, leaves, buds, and bird eggs.

Chimpanzees live in Africa. They are about the size of orang-utans. They spend as much time in the trees as on the ground, and are the smartest apes. They even use sticks to gather termites, and sometimes throw sticks at enemies. Besides termites, chimpanzees also eat fruit, leaves, and small animals.

Gorillas inhabit deep forests in Africa. Some of them weigh more than 600 pounds. The male gorilla beats his chest to keep strangers away. Gorillas look very fierce and are enormously strong, but they are usually peaceful and eat only plants.

CHIMPANZEES groom each other as monkeys do.

Young CHIMPANZEES run and play with each other for hours.

CHIMPANZEES usually walk on all fours, but can walk upright.

CHIMPANZEES have learned human sign language. Some of them know hundreds of "words."

25

DEER live in many places, including mountains, deserts, plains, and swamps. The males of most kinds have antlers. Except for the caribou, no female deer has antlers. Each year the antlers, which are made of bone, fall off and new ones grow to replace them.

MOOSE are the largest of all deer.

CARIBOU, or reindeer, are tamed to pull sleds.

Musk DEER have no antlers but have 3-inch tusks.

White-tailed DEER are from 2 to 3½ feet high at the shoulder.

The two-humped Bactrian CAMELS live in Asia.

GIRAFFES are the tallest of all animals— up to 18 feet tall.

Arabi CAME. (dromedari have one hun

GIRAFFES are very tall and have long necks and tongues. They can reach leaves on top of tall trees. When giraffes drink, they spread their front legs wide apart and bend their heads down to the water. With their long legs, they can run fast over the African plains.

CAMELS are useful in the desert because they can go for days without water. Their humps are full of fat which their bodies use when food is scarce. Camels can carry loads of up to 500 pounds. Their wide feet keep them from sinking into the sand and their nostrils can close to keep sand out.

HIPPOPOTAMUSES often yawn, showing their teeth as a warning to keep other hippos from bothering them.

HIPPOPOTAMUSES

HIPPOPOTAMUSES spend more time in the water than on land, especially in the daytime when the air is hot. Baby hippos learn to swim before walking and even nurse under water. Hippos sometimes float near the surface with only their nostrils, eyes, and ears showing. At other times, they walk on the bottom of the lake or river, or lie among the water plants, staying under for several minutes. Sometimes a mother hippo gives her baby a ride on her back in the water. After dark, hippos leave the water and go ashore to graze.

Hippos live in many parts of Africa.

Indian RHINOCEROSES have thick skin with deep folds. It looks like bumpy armor.

RHINOCEROSES

RHINOCEROSES are the only land animals that have horns on their noses, not on their foreheads. African rhinos have two horns, Indian rhinos one horn, and East Indian rhinos one or two. The horn is made of the same kind of material as your fingernails.

Because they are attacked by biting flies, rhinos like to roll in mud. The mud dries on their skin. This mud coat protects them from the flies and the mud bath cools them.

A rhino's sense of hearing and smell are good but it can't see very well.

ELEPHANTS are the biggest land animals today. They must eat great amounts to feed their huge bodies. Some elephants may eat about 500 pounds of leaves, roots, grass, and fruit and drink about 50 gallons of water a day.

An elephant drinks by sipping water into its trunk, which is really a very long nose, then squirting the water into its mouth. Elephants like water and often bathe in streams and ponds. They fill their trunks with water and spray it over themselves. The trunk is a built-in snorkel. An elephant can duck its head under water and still breathe by putting the tip of its trunk above the surface. During droughts, elephants dig for water with their feet.

The Asian elephant's back bumps up in the middle.

An Asian elephant's ears are much smaller than its head.

ASIAN elephants live in the forests and on the plains of southern Asia. Generally somewhat smaller than the African elephants, they are seldom more than 10 feet tall at the shoulder.

Female Asian elephants do not have tusks. Only some of the males have tusks, which usually measure less than 8 feet long.

When they take long trips, wild Asian elephants march in single file.

Asian elephants were trained thousands of years ago as work and riding animals. They are still used for hauling giant logs, some weighing as much as 2 tons, in the jungle. In some Asian countries, trained elephants are decorated with headdresses and ornaments and take part in parades and processions.

Asian elephants are the kind used in circuses.

The trunk is a very useful nose. Elephants use their trunks to help them eat, drink, and do lots of hard work.

only one "finger" at the end of the trunk

A newborn elephant weighs about 200 pounds. It has soft, fuzzy hair at birth but soon loses most of it. A one-day-old can walk for miles.

An African elephant's ears are as big as its head.

The African elephant's back dips in the middle.

Tusks are upper front teeth grown to a huge size. An African elephant's can be up to 11 feet long.

two "fingers" at the end of the trunk

AFRICAN elephants live in parts of Africa south of the Sahara Desert. Some live mostly on the plains, others in the forests. The elephants of the plains—called "bush elephants"—generally are the biggest. Really large ones reach a height of 13 feet at the shoulder and weigh about 7 tons. Most, however, are smaller.

Most male and female African elephants have tusks. Their ears are very large, sometimes bigger than a tall man. The huge ears serve as fans that keep the air around them moving, helping keep the elephant cool on a hot day.

African elephants often pull down or push over big trees to get at and eat hard-to-reach leaves. Sometimes they also eat bark from trees.

African elephants are hard to tame, so seldom have been used as work or riding animals.

The ARCTIC HARE has shorter ears than most hares.

The COTTONTAIL lives in North and South America.

The white-tailed JACKRABBIT travels 20 feet in one leap.

The EUROPEAN RABBIT lives underground in warrens.

The PIGMY RABBIT is only about 11 inches long.

RABBITS and HARES are cousins.

They look similar, but rabbits have shorter ears and hind legs, and smaller feet. Rabbits cannot run as fast as hares.

Rabbits live in underground burrows and that's where the babies are born. Newborn rabbits are helpless. They have no fur and cannot see.

Hares don't live in burrows, but hide in the brush or other vegetation. A newborn hare has lots of fur and wide-open eyes and can hop around minutes after it is born. In the winter, some hares' coats turn white and blend with the snow.

The PANGOLIN rolls up into a ball for sleep or for protection.

The AARDVARK uses its very strong claws to break down anthills.

The GIANT ANTEATER is sometimes 6 feet long, end to end.

The ARMADILLO has a long, sticky tongue like an anteater's.

ANTEATERS, pangolins, aardvarks,

and armadillos are some of the animals that feed largely or entirely on ants. Most of them have long snouts and small mouths. Their salivary glands produce sticky saliva that coats their long tongues, so they can easily lick up ants. With their powerful claws, they can break into anthills and termite nests. These animals are often toothless or almost toothless. The giant armadillo, however, has 100 little peg-like teeth (more than any other land mammal) which it loses as an adult. Armadillos have a hard shell for protection.

The PRAIRIE DOG gets its name from its barking sound.

The CHIPMUNK can hold nuts in its cheek pouches.

The JERBOA is a leaping desert rodent.

No! BATS are not flying rodents, though they look as if they might be. They are a group by themselves. Bats are the only mammals that can actually fly.

The MUSKRAT lives mostly in the water. It eats water plants, fish, and frogs.

The PORCUPINE, if threatened, turns and points its quills at the enemy.

The BEAVER is a good swimmer, with waterproof fur and webbed hind feet.

The FLYING SQUIRREL doesn't really fly— it just glides.

The SQUIRREL buries acorns to eat next winter.

The BLACK RAT eats the same things people eat.

The WOODCHUCK is also known as the groundhog.

The HAMSTER is now a favorite pet for children.

The HOUSE MOUSE lives where people choose to live.

The DEER MOUSE lives in woodlands or in meadows.

RODENTS live everywhere in the world except in the area around the South Pole, the Antarctic. More than one third of all kinds of mammals are rodents. There are runners, diggers, gliders, climbers, and swimmers among them. All of them have one thing in common: their unusual arrangement of teeth. The upper and lower front ones, called incisors, slant forward; then there's a big gap between them and all the other teeth. The front teeth gnaw off little bits of food, then the food is chewed by the back teeth. Rats use their teeth to gnaw through metal walls and even cinder blocks.

AUSTRALIA became separated from other continents millions of years ago. Now its mammals aren't like those of the rest of the world. Almost all are marsupials, whose females have pouches.

The BANDICOOT has ears like a rabbit's. It is about as big as a house cat.

KOALAS, which look like teddy bears, usually eat the leaves of eucalyptus trees.

a koala's unusual forepaw

WOMBATS spend all day underground in long tunnels that they dig. At night they come out to feed on grass and leaves.

NUMBATS use their long, thin, sticky tongues to gather up termites, their favorite food. A numbat eats 10 to 20 thousand termites a day.

The KANGAROO is the most familiar marsupial of them all. It has tiny forelegs but such powerful hind legs that it is able to leap 25 feet in a single bound. What a ride for the baby!

When frightened, a young kangaroo will rush back to its mother's pouch.

MARSUPIALS are born tiny and weak. They are totally helpless, much more so than newborn kittens or puppies or even baby mice. For many weeks, sometimes months, a marsupial baby lives and develops attached to its mother's nipple, from which it gets milk. The nipples of most marsupials are in the pouch which shelters the baby.

Most marsupials live in Australia. They were there when Australia became a separate continent 60 million years ago. Few other animals lived there, so marsupials thrived.

The kangaroo is the biggest marsupial, yet at birth it is only one-third of an inch long. Some kangaroos grow to be 9 feet long, including the tail, and may stand 6 feet tall.

Koalas live most of the time in eucalyptus trees, where they feed on leaves. A koala's forepaw looks like a hand with two thumbs.

The numbat is the size of a big squirrel. It has no pouch. The numbat catches termites and rats with its very long tongue.

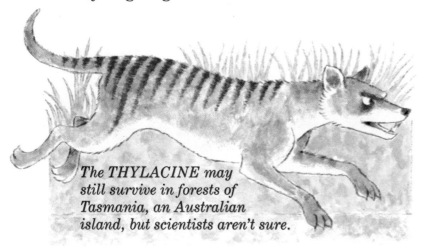

The THYLACINE may
still survive in forests of
Tasmania, an Australian
island, but scientists aren't sure.

The thylacine looks like a striped dog. It has a yard-long body and a tail almost 2 feet long. It hunts animals such as small kangaroos, birds, and reptiles. Years ago ranchers feared thylacines would kill their sheep. They destroyed so many thylacines that there may not be any left.

There are many kinds of bandicoots. Some have large hind legs and small forelegs, like kangaroos.

Wombats are about 36 inches long. They look like small bears and have coarse, thick fur and almost no tail. The front teeth of the wombat look like those of a beaver and are used for gnawing. The wombat's pouch opens backwards.

Some other marsupials are boodies, dibblers, dunnarts, noolbenders, potoroos, and quokkas.

Opossums live in North and South America. They are the only marsupials living outside Australia and the islands near it. When baby opossums leave the pouch, they ride on their mother's back. If an opossum is cornered by an enemy, it sometimes plays dead and waits for the enemy to leave.

MONOTREMES are the only mammals that lay eggs. There are only two, the platypus and the echidna. Both the monotremes are Australian.

A PLATYPUS is almost 2 feet long, with glossy fur. It has a leathery, duck-like bill, short legs with webbed feet, and a flat tail. It eats very small water animals. The female lays 2 to 3 eggs at a time. The babies lap up milk from small openings in the mother's belly. She has no nipples.

An ECHIDNA is covered with fur and sharp spines. The echidna is a very good digger. It catches ants and termites with its long tongue. The female has a fold of skin called a temporary pouch for her eggs and young. The young feed like platypus babies. When the young leave, the pouch shrinks and then disappears.

HORSES were tamed about 5,000 years ago in Asia.

GOATS were first tamed about 7,000 years ago in Iran. They have beards and curved horns.

Some CATTLE are descendants of the huge wild oxen called the aurochs, now extinct.

SHEEP were first domesticated about the same time as goats.

PIGS, domesticated wild boars, were used to round up cattle.

DOMESTIC ANIMALS started
out as wild animals, but they were bred and changed so they could be used by people. Cattle, sheep, goats, pigs, rabbits, chickens, and ducks were domesticated as sources of food or clothing. Horses, oxen, donkeys, burros, and camels were domesticated to pull wagons and to carry heavy loads and riders.

Dogs, cats, guinea pigs, hamsters, gerbils, and mice were domesticated to be household pets.

Because people controlled mating between domestic animals, many different types were developed. Today, some kinds of pigs are lean and tall, others are fat and short. Farm horses are huge and stocky, while racehorses are long-legged and sleek. Some cattle have been bred mostly for meat, others for milk. Sheep and goats are raised for milk, meat, and also for wool.

IBEXES, wild cousins of domestic goats, are sure-footed and live on mountain crags.

ZEBRAS live in many parts of Africa. They travel in herds.

CAPE BUFFALOS weigh up to 2,000 pounds and are very fierce.

WART HOGS have bumpy faces and large upper and lower tusks.

BARBARY SHEEP are not really sheep but are related to both sheep and goats.

WILD ANIMALS roam the earth, although their numbers are shrinking because humans are destroying their natural homes. There are many more kinds of wild animals than domestic ones.

Some wild animals are related to domestic ones. The ibex is a wild goat that lives in the high mountains of Africa, Asia, and Europe. It lives on plants with very tough leaves. The ancient Egyptians tamed some ibexes, but now all ibexes are wild.

The zebra, a striped relative of the horse, has never been domesticated.

Wart hogs are wild pigs of Africa. They live in burrows and kneel to eat grass.

Barbary sheep, also called aoudads, are related to sheep. They live in North Africa.

The African buffalo is a huge, fierce wild ox. It is sometimes called the water buffalo because it likes to be near wet places.

35

Horses are taught to perform with perfect timing.

The tiger act needs a brave, patient trainer.

a sea lion band

Circus people say that the most difficult animals to train are the bears.

36

Female elephants are easier to train than males.

The trained lion usually won't bite.

Apes and monkeys sometimes are dressed up as people.

Trained dogs do lots of tricks, like walking on their hind legs or forelegs or performing in a balancing act.

TRAINING ANIMALS to perform in the circus is a difficult and often dangerous task. Tigers and lions—"big cats" as they are called— sometimes attack their trainers.

Trainers first watch their animals to learn their abilities. If a big cat balances easily, it is taught to sit up or walk a tightrope. A good jumper is taught to leap through a hoop.

A sea lion's balancing tricks are based on its own natural characteristics. When a sea lion chases a fish through the water, it has to turn and twist its head very quickly to follow the fish. The same ability is used when a sea lion balances a ball on its nose. It must keep moving its head under the ball. It may take as long as six months for a sea lion to learn to balance a ball, a year for it to learn to stand on its flippers, and two years for it to learn to play a musical instrument.

Chimpanzees learn quickly and seem to like to imitate people. It may take them only a few days to learn tricks that other animals need months, at least, to master.

The easiest trick for a dog to learn is sitting up. The dog is steadied by a stick held under its chin.

Elephants are very intelligent and can learn many tricks. In a parade each elephant learns to put its forefeet on the back of the elephant ahead of it.

Horses trained to carry circus riders go around the ring with the same number of steps each time. This permits a rider who has to jump on and off a horse with split-second timing to know just where it will be at every moment.

How to train a bear to ride a bicycle.

Bicycle cannot move. Bear tries holding handlebars.

Learning to get on bike and to pedal takes bear 3 months.

Bear is now ready for moving bike. Trainer helps balance it.

At last bear can ride bike. Tired trainer is very happy.

A bird's streamlined body is designed to fly. Its hollow bones are light and its legs fold tightly in flight.

lung

sacs

When a bird flies, it uses lots of energy and its body heats up.

Air in balloon-like sacs attached to the lungs cools the body.

bird's thumb and fingers

bird's wrist

bird's elbow →

rib cage

bird's heel

bird's knee

bird's toes →

Beneath the layers of feathers, skin, and muscles is the bird's skeleton— it looks much like that of a person, with fingers, elbows, rib cage, knees, heels, and toes.

your wrist

your thumb and fingers

your elbow

your rib cage

Look, Ma! I'm a bird!

your heel

your knee

your toes

Here you are, trying to stand like a bird. But your short toes can't grasp a branch and your featherless arms make poor wings.

The 8,600 bird species come in many sizes.

The biggest bird is the ostrich (weight 300 pounds, 8 feet tall).

The smallest is the bee hummingbird (weight 1/10 ounce, 2¼ inches long).

A bird's beak is suitable for its eating habits.

Woodpeckers peck for insects under tree bark.

Pelicans scoop up fish.

Parrots can crack nuts.

Cardinals are seed-eaters.

A bird's feet, too, are suited to its needs.

perfect perching foot

big claws on hunting foot

webbed swimming foot

ALL BIRDS have two legs, two wings, a beak, and feathers, but they don't all look alike. There are over 8,600 different kinds of birds and one kind may look very different from another.

A bird's looks tell a lot about the way it lives. A mallard duck is a water bird. It has webbed feet for swimming and a broad bill for getting food from the water. The ostrich has long, powerful legs and, for its size, small wings. It does not fly like most birds but travels on the ground. It can run more than 30 miles an hour across the flat plains where it lives. The penguin cannot fly either. Its wings are like flippers, and it uses them to swim rapidly through the sea.

Herons, which live near water, have spindly legs for wading in the shallows, where they hunt for fish, frogs, and other small water animals. They catch these with their long pointed beaks. Vultures and eagles have broad wings for soaring high in the air while they look for food.

Some kinds of birds lay more eggs than others. Some penguins lay only 1 egg. Some bobwhites lay 24 eggs.

All birds hatch from eggs and egg size is related to bird size. The eggs of some hummingbirds are only about one-third of an inch long. An ostrich egg is about 7 inches long. It would take the contents of 24 chicken eggs to fill one ostrich egg.

Each kind of bird has its own type of nest. The megapode builds a huge mound of soil, sticks, and leaves, and lays its eggs within the heap. The razorbill doesn't build a nest at all but just lays its egg in a rock crevice. The oriole makes a big basket that hangs from a branch, while the hornbill nests inside a hole in the tree. The tern makes its nest in the sand of the beach and the phoebe nests under the eaves of buildings. High up on a treetop or cliff a bald eagle builds a very heavy 8-foot wide nest of branches and twigs, while down below a hummingbird builds a tiny 1-inch nest made of the softest plants and spider webs it can find.

Most birds choose a mate when it is time to start a family. The male tries his best to attract a female.

After mating, most birds will build their nests in a very safe place to prepare for their coming family.

The mother bird lays the eggs. Here she sits on them to keep them warm. The father bird guards the nest.

Soon the eggs hatch. The parent birds feed the babies until they can fly from the nest and feed themselves.

swallow

canary

When a bird's wings move up the feathers separate to let the air pass through so as not to stop the bird's forward movement.

scarlet
tanager

wood thrush

blue jay

bald eagle

mallard duck

Up! Up! and away!

People have made many attempts
to fly like birds by flapping
artificial wings. They have
never been very successful.

Shucks!

robin

When a bird's wings move down the feathers are together and tilted at just the right angle to push the bird forward.

starling

woodpecker

cardinal

oriole

thrasher

crow

bluebird

magpie

BIRDS FLY by flapping their wings up and down. Strong muscles are needed especially for the downstroke, which requires great thrust. The wing itself has hardly any muscle; the chest muscles move the wing. The chest muscles may sometimes make up half a bird's weight. Feathers are lightweight and strong, and give birds a smooth body form that cuts down on the drag of the air.

When a bird flaps its wing down, the big feathers on the outer half of the wing (called primaries) close, like the slats of a Venetian blind pulled flat. The wing pushes down against the air, lifting the bird. At the same time, the wingtip moves in a semicircle, down and forward, and wingtip feathers pull the bird ahead. During the upstroke, the primary feathers open, allowing air to pass between them, and wingtip feathers push back against the air, shoving the bird ahead.

Flying by flapping the wings takes lots of energy. Birds can also travel through the air without moving their wings by gliding. They can stay aloft by gliding because of the shape of the wing. It is curved out on top and in underneath. As the bird glides forward, its wing splits the air. Some air passes over the top, some under the bottom. The air flowing over the curved top of the wing has more distance to travel, so it moves faster. Air passing underneath moves slower. What this all adds up to is that there is less air pressure over the wings than underneath, and that means more push up than down.

A bird glides until gravity and the air's drag slows it down and it must land or flap its wings. Some birds can soar for hours on rising currents or air without landing or flapping their wings.

These birds can't fly. Neither can the ostrich or the emu. Their ancestors could fly, but these birds changed. Now their small wings can't lift them off the ground.

cassowary

penguin

kiwi

41

The ANHINGA is the only bird that can spear a fish. The fish is then tossed into the air so that it lands headfirst in the bird's mouth.

WEAVER BIRDS weave their nests with the entrance at the bottom to protect their families from the rain.

An EGYPTIAN VULTURE throws a stone on an ostrich egg until it breaks. The egg makes a meal.

Japanese fishermen used CORMORANTS to fish for them. The birds caught the fish under water, then brought it to the boat. The fishermen gave them a share.

OXPECKERS feed on insects they find on the backs of big animals—rhinoceroses and others.

The bird that can walk as fast as a man can run is the SECRETARY BIRD, a useful killer of dangerous snakes.

WONDERFUL BIRDS of many

kinds live almost everywhere in the world, from the tropics to polar climates. There are birds that walk, run, swim, and fly. Some birds have short, sleek feathers and others have big plumes. Some birds fly higher than Mount Everest and others live on the sea. Some birds fly over 2,000 miles without stopping. Many birds can find their way at night by the stars. Some birds can fly 100 miles an hour, and the amazing hummingbird can fly backwards or straight up or can hang in front of a flower without seeming to move, its wings a fast-beating blur.

some birds with unusual headdresses

blue-crowned pigeon

bulbul

touraco

umbrella bird

cockatoo

hoopoe

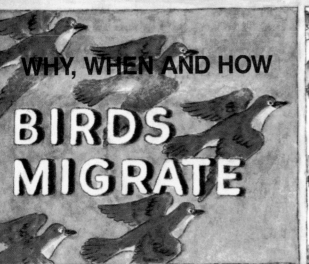

WHY, WHEN AND HOW
BIRDS MIGRATE

In late summer through early fall birds begin to migrate—fly to warmer climates. They migrate to escape from the cold winter weather when food is very scarce.

Oh, no!

They stay in warmer climates until spring, then fly home, ready to start new families.

Hi!

Some birds migrate alone...

some in   small groups...

and some in large flocks.

There are birds that do not migrate to warm climates.

blue jay   cardinal

These stay-at-homes work hard all winter to find food.

Most birds that live in the tropics never migrate.

birds of   paradise

It never gets too cold, so they stay where they are.

The migrating champion, the Arctic tern, flies from the North Pole area to the South Pole area and back every year.

1ST PRIZE

YOU TOO CAN BE A
BIRD WATCHER

If you want to watch birds in your back yard, you must attract them with food. Here are some of the kinds of bird feeders.

BIRD SEED

Birds need water to drink and bathe in.

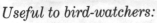

Useful to bird-watchers:

guidebook to identify birds

BIRDS

notebook to keep records of birds

binoculars for faraway watching

Some bird-watchers also keep photo records of birds they see.

When winter comes it is hard for birds to find food. Your feeder will help them.

These animals and many others are vanishing speci[...]

THE FUTURE

is hard to predict, but it is certain that unless people help them, some kinds of animals will vanish forever. Right now many animals are in danger of extinction.

Of course, throughout the millions of years animals have existed, many kinds have become extinct. Mostly, they disappeared from natural causes. Some, for instance, could not cope with changing climate. Usually, these vanished animals were replaced by new ones.

Today, it is different. Almost all the animals that are endangered are threatened by people and their activities. The problem is that the number of people is increasing rapidly. More people need more land on which to live and grow food. They need trees for building and firewood. They must dig for coal and drill for oil.

All of these activities destroy the places in which animals live. Without a place to live, an animal cannot exist.

...y are the animals that could very soon become extinct.

In some places, too, people are killing too many animals without leaving enough alive to continue their kind.

All, however, is not gloomy. Many people are working to conserve wildlife. Some zoos are breeding animals that are gone from the wild but remain in captivity. Many countries have stopped the killing of some rare animals. Most important, the wild places animals need to live in are being protected. If people stay concerned, wildlife can be saved.

Will all the animals be gone in the FUTURE and only people be left? Will zoos be places where people take turns looking at each other?

You are back in the days of the dinosaurs.
A Stegosaurus drops by and you offer it a snack.
Will it choose the juicy raw steak
or the branch of delicious tree leaves?
(See page 8.)

You are bird-watching out in the woods.
You come across woodpeckers, upright on
the trunk of a tree, banging their beaks
against it. What are they up to?
(See page 38.)

You are at the circus.
A bear is speeding around on a bicycle.
You are amazed, astonished, and astounded.
How are animals trained to do such tricks?
(See page 37.)